LIFE UN*edited*

Aditi Pandey

BlueRose Publishers
New Delhi • London

First Published in October 2021

ISBN: 978-93-5472-404-6

BLUEROSE PUBLISHERS

www.bluerosepublishers.com

info@bluerosepublishers.com

+91 8882 898 898

Cover Design:

Shreya Kapoor

Typographic Design:

Namrata Saini

Distributed by: BlueRose, Amazon, Flipkart, Shopclues

*Dedicated to: all the commoners who let the
Ordinary survive to procreate the Extraordinary.*

FOREWORD

I extend my congratulations to Ms Aditi Pandey for having pulled off a beautiful compilation of simple yet profound stories written lucidly with meaningful underlying themes. Her collection allows a peek into the lives of her characters derived from an ordinary world about us, punctuating the fundamental message that life is beautiful. In her stories, she tends to derive the 'extraordinary' out of the 'ordinary', something we unknowingly choose to ignore as we chase our busy schedules. 'Stop, think, relate and marvel' is what this collection prompts us to do.

In this book, the characters are well chalked out, from docile Rashmi to a patient Teysera, a dullard Mullu to the tough-looking Captain Sheron, who take the readers along a journey towards ultimate realization that it is the 'mundane' who matter. One of her stories tell us that in this world where people prefer to look through rose-tinted glasses and choose love marriages, Rashmi and Mullu find themselves tied together in an arranged marriage only to realize that love takes its own sweet time and stands beyond all apprehensions, stereotyped beliefs and labelled trends of the society. Similarly, another story about a feeble Teysera focuses on her unmatched mental strength.

The stories continue to present striking contrasts between the environments they're set up in, painting varied shades of human relationships with each other and nature. Each story finishes on a positive note, bringing out 'incredible' lessons affixed in 'routine' life. The multi-course meal of soul-satisfying stories go on and one wishes for them to never end.

I wish the author all the best for her future endeavors and hope that this book inspires others.

-   Kiran Nirvan
Bestselling author-duo of books like 21 Kesaris and The Kargil Girl

ACKNOWLEDGEMENT

I am highly indebted to Mr. Syed Arshad, Ms. Khushboo Kaushik and the whole team of BlueRose Publishers, Delhi, for bringing out this volume of my story book and for offering me this opportunity. I also express my gratitude to Mr Aditya Singh, Sr. Publishing Consultant and my Publication Manager, Bhanupriya for being prompt in responding to my calls and guiding me through.

Further, I express my profound gratitude to Ms. Chhavi Deshawal and Ms Jiya Pandey for providing me with beautiful sketches that have blown life into my stories and for their continued support in my literary pursuit.

I am greatly thankful to my respected Principal and school management for their guidance and support.

I also extend my gratitude to my dear friends and fellow teachers who have been a great motivation:

Ms. Ruchi Seth, Ms. Hemlata Matthews, Ms. Manju Mishra, Ms. Swarupa Dey, Ms. Rumna Banerjee, Ms. Shivani Kalra, Ms. Meeta Sinha, Ms. Kavita Pandey, Ms. Poonam Bhutani, Ms. Parveen Kaur Grover and Ms. Manju Taneja.

I am also highly grateful to all my students who have been a continuous source of vivacity in my life.

I EXPRESS MY LOVE AND GRATITUDE

To my family members: my husband Mr. Saurav Pandey, my daughter Jiya Pandey, my fur baby Cooper, my parents Mrs Pushpa Pandey Mr. Pradeep Kr. Pandey Mrs. Kamlesh Shukla Mr. Vinod Kr. Shukla, my brother Col Ankur Shukla, his spouse Lt. Col Arnavaz, their son Arhaan Shukla, my brother in law Gaurav Pandey, his spouse Mrs. Anuja and their son Shourya Pandey.

Aditi Pandey

E-mail: aditijiya27@gmail.com

PREFACE

I am an observer of life. Life that happens all around us, in even the smallest particle we see and being a voracious reader; I have tried to put my observations across through these stories that can be mighty life-changers for the readers.

This collection of stories allows a peek into the lives of a few ordinary people who show the striking reality that **Life is beautiful** and it is the mighty power of the **"Ordinary"** that creates the **"Extraordinary"**.

From the simple docile Rashmi to the patient Teysera, the drab Mullu to the Herculean Capt. Sheron, the readers shall journey along to a realization that it is the "Mundane" that matters. In this world of rose tinted glasses and love marriages, Rashmi and Mullu fell into the swamp of arranged marriage only to realize that love stands beyond all our fears, beliefs and the trends of the society. The physically meek Teysera showcases whacking mental strength. Magna has deep experiences to transform herself from a little girl with fears to a loving conservationist.

The stories continue to present striking contrasts from the harrowing fears to the varicoloured city of Kolkata this collection paints different shades of human relationships with other humans and Nature.

 Each story ends with a beautiful turn in the life of the protagonists leaving a message behind for the readers to **embrace the quotidian** as it is from this that the incredible burgeons.

Buy and gift the book to the people you love so that all embrace happiness.

I wish my readers BON VOYAGE! As they journey into the world of my stories.

Aditi Pandey

ABOUT THE AUTHOR

Aditi Pandey, currently working as a teacher at St. Mary's Convent Inter College, Lucknow has also worked as a Personality Development trainer and an IAS guest lecturer. Being a teacher by profession and also involved in Counseling, she has always been in touch with people of different ages, classes and beliefs. It is this that became her motivation to write... to write about the people who are struggling day in and day out to make a mark in this world. Aditi has thus, come up with this collection of short stories based on fictional characters as she believes that we are all heroes in our stories and need no Biopic to be the insignia of our perseverance and achievement. This happens to be her first published work though she has been friends with the pen since a long time where she has written articles poems and has also worked as a Content Writer. Pandey also holds the recognized post of the Editor-in-Chief of her school magazine and has been contributing regularly.

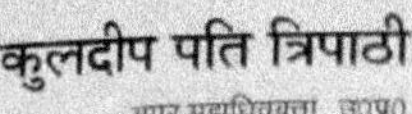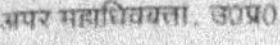

कुलदीप पति त्रिपाठी

अपर महाधिवक्ता, उ०प्र०

उच्च न्यायालय
लखनऊ पीठ लखनऊ

निवास	: 1ए, बसंत विहार पिकनिक स्पाट
	रोड, इन्दिरानगर, लखनऊ
फोन	: 0522–2722705 (का.)
	0522–2723253 (का.) 2722729
	0522–2715812 (आ.)
मो0	: 9415029053
ई –मेल	: kptripathi223@gmail.com

सं0 : ....

दिनांक : ....

FOREWORD

This book *"LIFE-UNedited"* by an upcoming author Ms. Aditi Pandey who is currently working as a teacher brings out the reality of life and beauty of different people from different backgrounds.

Its characters are very simple and common humans who work with uncommon elan in whichever field they are. This pure spirit of the myriads of characters depicts a pure Indian culture and tradition which is the striking feature along with the motivational message added at the end of each story.

I wish a lot of good luck to Ms. Pandey and would recommend this book to be read by each human so that we all learn the real art of living LIFE.

(Kuldeep Pati Tripathi)

CONTENTS

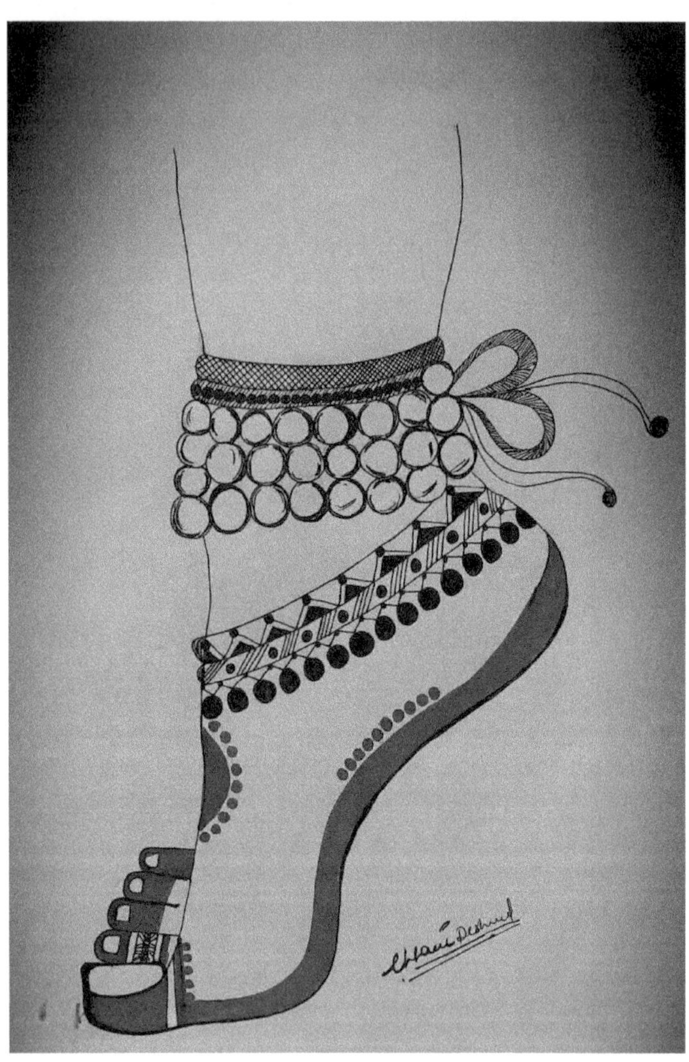

1. A STONE OF FLOUR

Working in the kitchen, wrapped in a cotton saree, Rashmi was in a hurry. Something made her move through the kitchen in a jiffy. Carrying the basket full of colourful vegetables, her face looked so pale that she looked no less than lovelorn. Suddenly, her husband entered the dining hall like a triumphant king telling her to serve the food. But Rashmi, who was not ready, trembled with fear. Rashmi had always been very petrified of her husband as he looked reserved and unsympathetic. She clung onto the gnawed edges of her "pallu" where her eyes met her tinkling varicoloured bangles which appeared to be no less than shackles that had kept her bound to the arranged marriage.

It had not been more than a week since Mullu and Rashmi had got married. Mullu was a hefty man, well-built and had a grim expressionless face. Since the time of the wedding Mullu had been very busy paying off the dues of the decorator, the caterer and the wedding planner. Today was the day when all had been cleared and Mullu got a sigh of relief as he sat in the lobby. Sitting in the lobby near the kitchen, this was the first time that Mullu examined Rashmi. Rashmi, a girl of 19 overladen with jewellery, all covered in the six yard looked like a wrapped gift sent on the wedding but beyond all this her red, teary eyes and innocent charm touched the man whose heart was made of flint and Mullu decided to help her. While Mullu had felt something for the first time he headed towards the kitchen. No one knows what it was. Was it pity or some attraction of a strong man whose heart was that of a child and craved to be loved or was it the moth in the form of a human who got allured towards the fiery red of Rashmi's saree?

On the other hand, fearing that the delay in the preparations of dinner may infuriate her strapping man, Rashmi planned to be quick and knead the flour. Rashmi who was not a dwarf but a short and sweet girl, ignorant of Mullu's presence behind her tried to reach to the flour container on the tip of her toes but the quivering hands did not support her much and as she was trying to pull the flour container from the rack overhead all the flour fell painting both Mullu and Rashmi milky-white.

The silence in House Number-100 Elgin Road, Kolkata was suddenly disrupted when the two burst into a laughter. Rashmi looked at the brawny man trying to hold the flour container in his sturdy arms to save her; he looked like a snowman with no muffler on and to her, he looked like the "Saviour". The one who was as pure as the white of the flour that covered him.

She realized that as human beings we make things difficult for ourselves by complicating life. Everything and anything can be sorted well with the weapon of laughter. The marriage which was arranged by the parents and out of which Rashmi had no hope was not actually "ugly". The man she had not liked at all finding him to be very stony was the one she had the best laugh with.

We must remember to revel in the joy of living life as it comes without judging, assuming or creating a fear of the unknown.

THE
GURKHA

2. THE "INSIGNIA"

"2 hours to go", murmured the anxious Ms Ashlesha as she waited for the train she had to catch. It had not been a very pleasant experience for the youngster sitting at the station unable to find any congenial company. The debilitated girl was in a bad mood, still unable to find a perfect reason for which she had been asked to travel for an official work that too at such a short notice. And to worsen things more, she saw a lanky dog come and sit right in front of her spreading its spindly forelegs to make her feel more disgusted. Soon, the 2 hours went by and Ms Ashlesha boarded the train. By all the grace of God, she got an almost vacant bogie and the window seat. Ms Ashlesha felt that God was trying to make up for all that she had suffered at the station. Soon, the train moved thrusting in a gush of cold breeze that made her locks wave.

It was all this that she was mulling over when draughts of air caressed her cheeks. She gazed around and found nothing much interesting as a girl of 20. Peeping out of the train window she saw nature at its best but the berth opposite to hers was still vacant. She looked at the ebony coloured berth and felt as if loneliness had struck it. After a while as she felt a certain tranquility, she peeped out of the window and found the peaceful stars gleaming from amongst the cold patches of dark clouds colouring the blue sky. The young lady's thoughts were disturbed and all the impressions soon buckled under the arrival of a fellow passenger; when a large bag landed on the berth opposite to hers, with a thud. She looked up to find a bulky man with a colossal built sitting on that berth with the bag. He was as tall as a eucalyptus tree. She espied him and found him to be very unpleasant. "A *hefty* young man with a scar on his face", she thought. Soon it was time to detach the middle berth which was a challenge for the young girl. As we know; all good things come in small packages, but this time the small package that God had confined her soul in was a bit of a problem. The height factor with Ms Ashlesha was not letting her reach the upper berth to unhook the middle berth and the tall fellow quickly helped her. He seemed to be no less than a devil but at that very moment he seemed to be an angel in disguise and out of the human instinct, after an hour or so they introduced themselves. "I am Captain Sheron", he said. Suddenly, all the gratifying feelings changed. More than his name she was interested in the prefix. "An army personnel surviving on the discounted goods of the army canteen", a series of internal monologue started. After all she was one of the honest tax payers. Keeping her grievances aside she spoke to him and found out that he was returning home from his "border posting" at Poonj. They had a formal verbal exchange when she inquired more about his stay at Poonj. The man then went on and on like an arrow surging ahead and gave a lot of description. All this while, during this whole discourse upon how he would stay in the bunkers staying up the whole night; sometimes counting the stars, sometimes the bullets and sometimes the dead bodies of his fellow officers; what vexed her was the scar on his face. There was something unusual about it. It was a deep incision. It was for sure an old but serious injury. Though she was always known for her peaceful and non-violent behaviour yet it was just the scar that caught her attention recurringly. "You must have won many medals", she said to him casually; listening to so much on army but before she could complete, it was time for him to get down. He picked his bag and while he was about to go he turned, placing some sheaves of old newspaper in Ashlesha's hands and said, "I wear my medal on my face, madam. Have a safe journey ahead." She was stunned by his reply. Regaining her senses she turned the pages of the newspaper to read the headlines "In another Poonj encounter Capt. Sheron brought down two terrorists." She felt she was in some stupor. She read further only to find out how the man she met had been a hero to save little orphan kids from the clutches of a militant group while he was on a leave and how he had lost his 1 month old baby saving those parent-less kids. She could now join the dots and understand that the scar that caught all her attention was a cicatrix. What she could not decide was just the fact that whether it was an insignia of his valour and goodness or a mark that would always remind him of the heart-rending experience of losing his own kid. But for sure she understood that:

As a human being we are all born for a special purpose. Many of us are unable to identify the special purpose we are born for, we keep complaining all the time and remain skeptical about what the others do. We must remember that we must not be cynical rather try to approve each and every effort of every human as we never know who is going an extra mile for our betterment. The biggest truth of life is that even the smallest of our efforts and good deeds get recorded somewhere in this universe to be returned at the right time so we must just try to do all the good we can, wherever we can, in whatever way we can, by all the means we can.

3. STRUGGLE-REMAIN-RISE!

It was not out of choice but out of chance that Sona became a teacher by profession. The need for money and the attempt to make up for the so called "loss" of not getting a dowry as her husband quoted, made Sona start working as a trainer just 2 months after delivering her little angel. It was not easy but the little baby perhaps understood all in her mute silence and slept the entire evening enabling her mother to work for the evening shifts. Leaving her little darling with her own mother or her husband, Sona would venture out each day.

But the struggles Sona had to face were too many. Travelling by the auto, moving out of the house at 1:30 pm with scorching heat of the sun gaping its mouth wide open and the pangs of leaving her bundle of joy behind every day, it was a throbbing experience but Sona, courageously took a stride in the world yet unknown to her.

She joined the institute with a positive feel but it was not very easy as it was her first experience in the professional arena. Sona worked with all her heart to build herself as well as her students up. And as it is said when you work with love, your work loves you back; soon, she adjusted well and surged ahead, enjoying her work.

Every day, she returned from work at around 9:00 pm to an unsettled house and an eagerly waiting daughter. She would be work and travel stained but the little baby's angelic smile would infuse a new vigour in her. She was a cherubin in those days of struggle for Sona. And with the newly attained energy, Sona would chop vegetable for dinner as she fed her kid after a long gap of around eight hours. It would be the best reunion to see the mother and daughter together where the little baby babbled and the mother would comprehend all. After spending some half an hour with the apple of her eye, Sona would put her in the pram near the door that led to the kitchen to cook the further meal for her husband and herself.

All was manageable until the parent in laws came to stay with her for a few days. As Sona grew up in a typical Indian family she always had a lot of reverence for the in laws but generation gap infected the thoughts and created a ridge. A sore was created in her relationships back at home. As she was rising in her career, her relationships were getting estranged. The parents at home did not approve of the lady of the house to be out till so late, coming back home only to serve a meal at nowhere earlier than 10:30 pm. Tension grew as she returned to a not so happy old couple waiting for her. The hidden harsh sarcastic comments of the mother in law which she tried her best to ignore, kept echoing in Sona's mind all the time. But she knew the art of not mixing personal with professional.

One day at office, her hard work was identified and she was promoted to a higher post and grade. It was a handsome raise but for her, what mattered more was the regard the promotion would get for her. Sona felt ecstatic. She felt euphoric. She was thrilled by this beautiful piece of news and was exhilarated at the day's events. Happily she took an auto. She felt herself to be no less than the "grey-eyed" goddess Athena of Greek mythology. The auto her chariot and the auto-driver, the owl. The way to her house seemed to be longer, that day. Actually, her joy was too much for her to hold. She wanted to share it all with her family. And when we are happy, Phoebus' steeds seem to founder. She was growing impatient and all this made the journey to look like a more time taking affair. As she got down the auto, she paid a Rs. 20 note. Not having a tenner the auto driver asked for change but Sona was too happy to have waited for a tenner and like a bounteous queen, she asked him to keep the full 20. She rushed inside the house with her sweetest smile on her lips, her twinkling eyes, a bit of her messy locks that had borne the torture of strong winds as she had peeped out of the auto and with her sweat tainted face only to find both the parents waiting for her. Before she could share anything her father in law's statement came as a thunderclap when very solemnly he said, "Quit the job". The dome of heaven crashed for Sona. No one was to be blamed but this was not what she was heading to. She could not even share her happiness. As she tried to explain things to the parents in a subdued tone, she heard another sentence from her dad in law. It was more of a threat this time. He said, "Quit the job or leave the house." This prevented her from saying anything. There was a ridge in relationships, she knew but it would come to this; she had never thought. But by now, she had surely understood the fact that:

All the times we feel happy, we feel as if something has been achieved; there is definitely going to be someone waiting for us... to pull us behind, to steal all the thrill of standing apart, to shatter our dreams, to spoil all the good we have done, to show us down and to not let us be really happy. But Sona was not ready to give up. She knew this was her time, she knew she was not born to give up rather to be reborn again and again from her ashes as the world would try to burn her dreams repeatedly... sometimes, in the name of customs, sometimes in the name of loyalty, respect, tradition and God knows what all. She picked her daughter and once again, courageously took a stride in the world yet unknown to her, but this time her steps were confident and stable. She glided ahead without even bothering to find out if her partner, her mate would accompany her because she knew she would be enough for her baby who was born out of her flesh and her blood. She needed no one. She smiled as she looked at her wrist. She would still adorn the red bangles that tinkled as she walked away towards a world with more freedom but only until they became shackles for her.

Such is the world. If faced with such a situation hope you will be able to remain stable, to stay strong enough to recollect your shattered pieces and put them all together. Even if you cry it is OK... as those tears are very much a part of you just like your beautiful, shining, glittery smile. Just remember to stay and fight, as who would know more than you that the struggle is hard and harder is the survival but there's a reason why you did not quit till now...

So

Struggle -Remain-Rise!

কলকাতা

4. A SPECIAL LETTER

As I depart,

Dear Kolkata- I must tell you...

I am carrying a part of you along in the form of the trinkets, the kantha blouses, the sarees, the chhena sandesh that almost melted in my mouth every time I took a bite, the little droplets of your rain, the purity of the immaculate white Victoria Memorial, the tranquility of the Gangasagar, the blessings of the Kaalighat temple, the hues of the gariahaat, the cries of the sellers, the tinkle of the temple bells, flavours of the mishti dohi, and above all "lessons well-learnt". And am also leaving a bit of me behind- with the eunuck I gave a lift to, with the balloon seller I got balloons from, with the little "tinku" at the church entrance gate I smiled at every evening (despite being unknown to each other), with the lily flowers I clicked, the private taxi driver and above all in the way we embraced each other. I have never felt this kind of a connection with any other place but the lights gleaming on your Howrah Bridge did ignite a spark in my eyes a spark of joy and love. As the waves of your Hooghly River flowed freely so has flown my soul freely on the roads that you own. I shall cherish every moment of me being with you as you have unveiled life to me in its purest form. Through the smile of the "Amma" who sold flowers at the street and despite all the troubles and poverty always carried a wholesome smile, through the peddler who was never weary of calling out to people for his wares. Life brims in you and your people. There is an undying and untiring spirit in all that I saw. There is a special hue in your colours. I am carrying it all with me in my heart and will each day try to imbibe and instil the same spirit in my life. What this connection is I know not nor will I ever be able to give it a name but, it is indeed a pleasure to share that now you are an integral part of my being.

It is now time to say goodbye...

Be good...

Stay safe, till we meet next

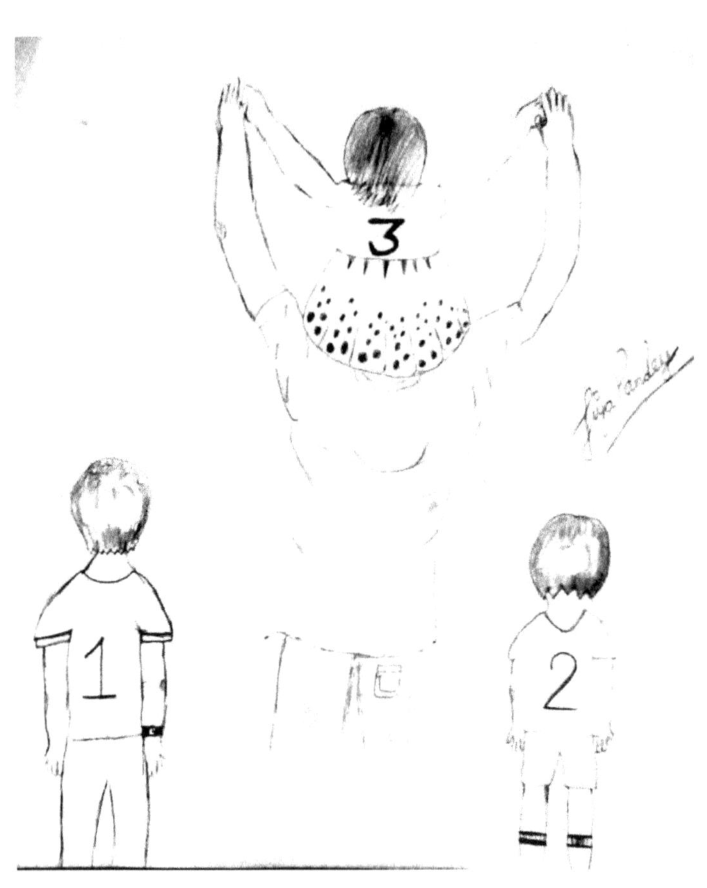

3
1
2

5. THE "TERZA"

"Three is such a jinxed number, and so are you!" said the grandmother as Teysera dropped the dish on the floor and soon the grey cemented floor turned reddish-yellow with pieces of "bhetki" scattered around. Bhetki" was not generally cooked in the house unless there was some esteemed guest about to visit the Dhaliwal family as it was a big deal to afford such a costly dish in the meal each day in a family with just one earning member. The yellow and red that signifies hope, love and joy reminded Teysera of all that was missing in her life. Listening to the hue and cry raised, Mother quickly rushed and picked up all the pieces of the costly fish to wash them off and re-prepare the entire dish.

Since the day she was born the whole family, excluding the mother had been very sad. The old grandmother had suggested in a solemn tone the idea of burrying the third born of the Dhaliwal family, the little cherubin born to Mrs Ange Dhaliwal. Teysera always used to feel very heartbroken and torn apart. Every time she heard such comments she felt bad till last year, but recently she had changed or maybe time had changed her. Listening to the same accusations, and remarks Teysara had perhaps become immune to all of them. She quietly apologized to mom and went to her room... or shall I say to her so called room. The little space under the stairs - the spandrel was her room. She went inside sat there and looked at the old dull red bricks with heaps of extra cement left here and there as if the mason had been in too much of hurry just like her father who had been in too much of hurry to love her or acknowledge her existence. She could connect so well. This little space under the staircase never got many visitors besides Teysera and a few rats or lizards. It was equally unwanted as this 'pretty' girl. Pretty not because she had good looks but because she had a strong and good heart. Soon her mother came looking for Teysera to call her for lunch. Bending and trying to enter the little hideout, she said, "How do you actually fit in here when there is such less space?" "The way I did fit in your womb mom, all cozy and protected though the world never wanted me", Teysera replied. There was utter silence. A kind of screaming silence and the mother kept looking at Teysera trying to take a plunge into her deep blue eyes but as usual what she found was only calmness. Mother had always tried to look for questions in Teysera's eyes but had never been able to find any. Maybe because Teysera knew very surely that mom really loved her.

Finally, they all sat to have lunch followed by the fruits session. Despite being a humble family, "The fruit session" was a ritual followed every day in the Dhaliwal family, every afternoon and as usual once again granny cut the apples and peeled them only to give all the pulp to Ardhan and Abhi, Teysera's elder brothers and all the peel to Teysera. She felt bad and the rage in her heart made her face reflect the red colour of the apple peel.

Soon 'bauji' entered silencing all. 'Bauji', Teysera's father who interacted only enough to drop Teysera to the government school in Hissar was a middle-aged dull man busy with the humdrum routine work. A three times appearing candidate at the NDA SSB once at Bhopal, then at Bangalore and finally at Allahabad; a seven times appearing candidate at the CDS SSB and a failure at all, Bauji landed up working as a clerk at the Railways. Since then he has been working there with his two elder sons studying in the railway schools while Teysera studying at a nearby government school. Every day Bauji would drop Teysera to the school not out of affection but for the fear of she doing something wrong that would cast a slur on the family name and this walk of around 10 minutes used to be full of silence "piercing silence" which was always broken by the rolling drumbeats that the duo heard as they moved past the marching soldiers while crossing the cantonment area. This was the only time when Bauji would smile in those 10 minutes. There would be something magical about the whole experience. The uniformed, organized, steady soldiers marching to the rhythm, the drum cadences, the high pitched voice commands, the synchronized swing of the arms, the heads held high in pride, the well adorned guns, the thudding feet ... it all would stir something within Bauji and this something was always well noticed by Teysera in the red teary eyes of her father. The bond between the father and daughter was not strong but yes as it is said "Blood is thicker than water" without saying anything she kept noticing everything. Soon, they would reach school and dropping his not so loved daughter at school Bauji went to his office.

Years went by and unlike the other two, Teysera kept passing her class every year with an average result. She reached college and after a lot of debating got the approval to pursue further studies. The entire debate rose as Bauji and grandma felt that all the fee-money could be saved for Teysera's wedding and the second problem was that she was required to go out of her village and stay in a hostel for her graduation. But mother tried hard and somehow Teysera was permitted to complete her B.Sc. Teysera had grown up and from her childhood she never had any good memory except for her mother's love and the look on Bauji's face every time the marching contingent was seen. All through her college days, as she was away from her family, she could never forget "that" what made her father happy. And so while appearing for her third year examination she also appeared for the written exam of OTA stealthily. Completing the graduation Teysera returned home and suddenly received a call letter for her SSB. The whole family was taken aback. Abhi said, "How will you do the excessively exhausting physical drills? You are so thin with an angular face." To which Teysera said, "Strength is not in your biceps and triceps but in the mind." Bauji looked unmoved and in a very hopeless and guttural tone he said, "I permit you to go and try your luck but Army is not meant for all." Teysera should have been happy but Bauji's statement broke her. She felt as if it was the ultimate crashing of Heaven's dome. She had expected a pat on her back from her father for her attempt, knowing what "Army" meant to him but nothing of this sort happened. She went on to appear for the interview and the medical, qualified it and soon joined as a "Cadet" at OTA Chennai. She was happy but one person was happier and that was her mother. Though her mother did not say much, the tight hug that Teysera got unraveled a hundred emotions. Teysera went for her one year training and did well. Back at home nothing had changed much. Bauji still did not talk to Teysera but yes he did inquire about Teysera's well-being every now and then from Ange. Finally, came the red letter day 9th March, 2019 when it was the Passing out Parade (POP) of 172 OTA officers and as it is customary the family of the cadets were invited. Forgetting everything Teysera only wished to see the "eyes" of her father as she would march in the ground to step on the "Antim Pag". And, it was time for the "Pipping Ceremony". Some miracle happened and out of the railway employee emerged Mr Dhaliwal who stepped forward like a triumphant victorious Commandant of a unit that had just won over the Tiger Hill again. Proudly, he moved ahead for the ceremony. The whole family accompanied and as Teysera changed to Lt. Teysera Dhaliwal with the stars on her shoulders shining -brightly the only other gleam to match this shine was the gleam in the red teary eyes of Bauji. Mother felt happy as it was a union she had always waited for. The family that once cried at the birth of this girl child, cried once again together but this time the tears were "Tears of Joy".

Teysera thanked granny. She said, "Granny thank you for making me feel that I was jinxed. Had you not done that, I would have never been able to do this." For the first time grandma had nothing to say and quietly gave her a peck on the cheek. Soon a waiter came to serve a platter of fruits. Grandma quickly picked up the apple to put it in the mouth of Teysera but she refused to have it saying, "I find the peel tastier than the pulp." All laughed and danced to the tunes of "Auld Lang Syne". As all were delighted mother once again tried to take a plunge into the deep blue eyes of Teysera to which Teysera replied, "It's all fine ma, I have no grudges, no complains. I am as strong as was the womb of the lady who bore me. I love you ma." The mother daughter duo then hugged and laughed.

Teysera had matured enough to understand that it is not the pale looking pulp like the comfortable life but the glossy red peel like the troubles of life that nourishes us and prepares us to step towards success.

And finally an overwhelmed Bauji exclaimed joyfully, "Nobody could do it,."

"Na Pehla, na dusra what has been done by 'Teysera'!"

6. AN ENCOUNTER WITH THE "NAWABS"

20ᵗʰ October, 2019 shall always be a special one. It was this very day that changed for me, the very motive of living. It was another usual evening. Winter was setting in and the eye of the day had started weakening. There was some strange heaviness in the atmosphere. The grey walls of the buildings, the dregs of moisture and the whole tiring day that I had had, all made life lustreless. As I reached home, my phone beeped. Expecting it to be my best friend's message, I felt music as well as colour returning to my boring Sunday but the myth broke breaking my dream; my long cherished dream to get an acceptance to join the crew of Page-3 reporters.

Dear Peculiari Hope

We are glad to announce your transfer to Lucknow and also inform you that you already have your first assignment "The Heroes" in which you are supposed to create a weekly report based on the four achievers from Lucknow who have worked in the army. We wanted the most capable one to take this project and you are our best that we have. You are supposed to take a flight tomorrow at 10 a.m. We are sending a copy of your ticket attached with this mail.

As I read the official mail from my Boss, I hunkered on the couch and felt no less than a swan to die of heartbreak. I looked around to see a small mosquito trapped in the web, wriggling continuously- a mirror image of myself. Collecting my shattered pieces, I got up to pack my bags and went off to sleep early that night. The next morning, after getting a few directions as to how the company would take care of shifting my stuff other than the clothes to Lucknow, I rushed to the airport. Finally, it was time to leave Mumbai but there were no pangs of separation. Only the pain of not being able to make it to page-3 reporting as Mumbai was the best location for page-3 reporters.

The flight took off while I silently wept myself off to sleep under the eye mask. It took me 2hrs 20min. to reach the Chaudhary Charan Singh Airport at Lucknow. I moved out like a not so happy gorilla who is dragged to the cage while my mind kept playing the advocate presenting arguments "Why can't they give me Page-3? I am so perfect to do page -3 pretty, smart, bubbly, vivacious. I have worked so well and if we go by their words, I am their best. Moreover why Lucknow? I mean it is such a small city. " Suddenly, I saw my name board in the drivers hand and my advocate rested his case. I was lodging at a hotel called Ramada a little away from the airport. I was greeted well and the ambience of the hotel was good. Mr Bose had always taken care of providing good accommodation. So this had to be my home sweet home until I got a rented one. It was a Saturday when I had reached Lucknow-the city of Nawabs. I had two days to move around before I began with my work. The manager, a lanky fellow stood opposite me putting entries in his system. Seeing me, he thrusted sheaves of paper in my hand and asked the bellboy to escort me to my room. The sheaves were nothing but a travel brochure kind of a thing. "What could be worth a sight-seeing plan in such a town", I thought to myself and not very eager and interested, I thought of hitting a few places.

I checked in, freshened up and moved out to explore Lucknow – the city of "NAWABS" where I was very sure, none existed anymore. With a grin, I could recall all the crime cases of Lucknow that I had heard of from our crime reporting department Lucknow head, Mr. Misra who happened to be a family friend. I do not know if it was a blessing or a curse to be from a family that had seen many reporters and their reporter friends. Not willing to get into a trap of my extremely skeptical and inquisitive mind, I quickly drew my attention to the brochure in my hand.

The first place in the brochure was "The Bara Imambara" it also had a funny name to it "Bhool Bhulaiya". So I decided to get my funny bone tickled and decided to visit this one first. I soon reached and met a fellow who claimed to be the official guide. While I was trying to get the details from the brochure he asked, "May I help you, madam? I shall explain the whole story and tell the detail." I was a bit sceptical that he may act as an extortionist yet I accepted his proposal. "What would you charge?" "Whatever you feel like madam if my work pleases you though the rate is Rs.500"; having said this, he pointed towards the rate board. Then he started, "The building you see madam is a majestic structure. It includes the large and beautiful Asfi mosque, the labyrinth, Bowli- a well with steps and running water and two impressive gateways that would lead the visitors to the main hall. You may be surprised to know that there are around 1024 ways to go to the terrace but to come back, only one". As he went on, my interest kept growing. "The roof", he said, "is made up from the rice husk." "And yet it has stood the ravages of time", I wondered. Not just this, he also offered and not just offered rather insisted on me to take a few pictures that would be a priceless memory. I agreed and did pose. It was here that I felt the cold breeze which seemed to have come to embrace me and hug me. I remembered mom's last few words, "Every time you feel the strong wind it will be me hugging you". My guide took me all through and finally it was time for me to pay him. I wanted to experiment and gave him 350/-. He took the money touched it to his forehead, kissed it and said, "I will work more on my explanatory skills, madam." It was here that I noticed his wrinkled face which had been the abode to his pure, gleaming eyes; his thin body; his bent back, he was a bit bent don't know if it was because he didn't follow the rules of right posture or because he had a lot of responsibilities on his shoulders. His soft smile was no less than the jasmine flowers that were in full bloom in the garden of the Imambara; which are though tiny yet the fragrance they spread is unmatchable. Involuntarily, I pulled out a Rs. 500 note and gave it to him he quickly put his hand in the pocket to return the earlier 350/- that I had given to him. Having an apprehension that such a thing might happen, I had started moving by then and only turned to say, "Your skills are amazing and so are you, Karim-Sikhiy." That was his name that I had read from the name tab of his. I felt a sudden kind of elation and a smile ran across my lips. I don't know if it was happiness, contentment, my mom's company that I had felt or the soft smile of Karim that had infected me.

A little happier, a little lighter and too hungry, I moved ahead to reach the famous Tundey Kebab stall next. This one I had really read a lot about on the internet and being too hungry, I placed my order. Soon a platter full of kebabs was placed before me with a bowl of green "chutney" and as I started to eat the kebabs, I found them too be a real treat. They were so soft that every bite seemed to melt in my mouth spreading the strong flavours of garlic, onion, ginger, clove, black pepper, nutmeg, bay leaf, cinnamon and what not. Every morsel seemed to take away all my exhaustion and apprehension. Paying my bill and a tip to the waiter, I came to the hotel and slept like a log only to be woken up by a symphony of the "Azaan" and temple bells. Very much unlike the noise of vehicles that used to be my alarm in the earlier city. I planned to start work that day. And pulled out the list of names of the officers for my venture "The Heroes"

1. Late Major Ritesh Sharma
2. Late Capt. Manoj Pandey
3. Late Lt. Hari Singh Bihst
4. Late Subedar Kevlanand
5. Late Rifleman Suneel Jang Mahat

As I read the names I found one thing that stayed common with every name – the word "LATE". Soon I started doing my ground work. While in this process I met an auto driver, Asharfi Lal who helped me a lot not only with the travelling but also in finding a rented house for me. It was the house of Mr. Shukla whose only son was serving in the armed forces. Both Mrs and Mr Shukla were so innocent that they readily accepted me as a part of their family and had long conversations telling me about their son who was away somewhere at the front. Spending time with them I understood that their whole life revolved around their only son. And one day I asked Mrs Shukla, "Don't you miss your son?" "No not at all just that our calendar is little different from what the others have." I could not understand and seeing me perplexed, she said, "All our festivals only come with the arrival of my son. Every time he is back on a leave we celebrate all –Holi, Diwali, Rakshabandhan, Christmas, Eid and so on…" . Of course her eyes were a little moist. "Why did you send him you had only one?", I asked. "My one can save thousands, how could I not have?", she said; making me dumbstruck.

I further went on to visiting the houses of the four martyred officers. Every house was just a humble middle-class family home that had been built with a lot of dreams. The parents of all these officers were so simple, meek and normal and I kept wondering from where they managed to get so much of courage to talk of their biggest loss and with tears in their eyes, take pride in what their sons had done. It was a great interaction with the family members of "The Heroes" and I was finally able to complete my report on "The Heroes".

It was now time for me to leave Lucknow. This time things were little different somehow, I had become fond of this city. But there were no pangs of separation as perhaps it was a bond beyond any boundaries that I had built with this town in those 8 months that I had spent here and I knew that I shall carry this city and its people in my heart forever.

I also had the realisation that the Nawabs did survive even today. They survived in men like Karim-Sikhiy, whose name meant generous and so he was; that's what Nawabs are. The Nawabs did exist in Asharfi Lal, who though had an unimpressive appearance with his hair erect like the reeds on an infertile land, his habit of chewing beetle all the time yet so helpful. The Nawabs can be found even today in the kebabs of Aminabad and the hospitality of people like Mrs and Mr Shukla and in all those soldiers who like true Nawabs sacrificed their own life to protect their kingdom and people.

It was from there that the very motive of my life changed. I became the part of the editorial team to bring up the long lost culture, tradition and richness of such towns which have way more to offer than the superficially glamorous Page-3 lives of the big cities. I felt I was born to take up this "Special" task and so I was named by my parents...

Peculiari Hope which meant Special Hope!

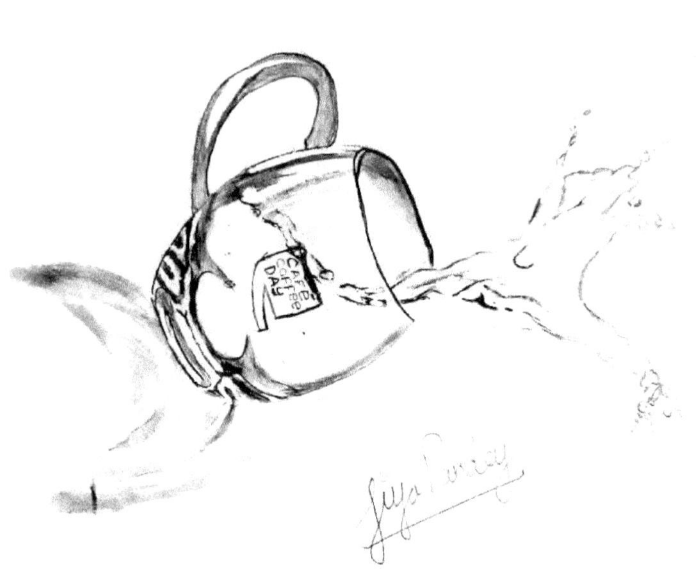

7. RIP!

"Sit straight it's a class, we are not hanging out in CCD"

As a teacher I often used this statement to check the body posture of my students… Why, I know not but perhaps the reason was that Café Coffee day was one of the most happening café of those days. And one fine day as I sat with my huge mug of coffee as black as the world of Pluto or Hades, I read the shocking news. "V G Siddhartha, the CCD owner commits suicide." Reading about Mr V G Siddhartha… what hovered over me was just the thought that what could have gone so wrong with CCD? What made things so crooked for CCD- a name that had been straightening my children's posture.

What was it that the one who served happiness in almost every cup with a smiley floating on the white, frothy surface of tasty coffee… felt life to be so insipid that he decided to end it…?

Perhaps it is **the reality** that stays left out, left behind in the so called cosy-protected spaces, we provide to our kids. It is high time we realize the need to make our children learn to hear a NO, accept their follies and take their DEFEATS. We must understand MONEY is not everything… It comes, it goes but we must STAY… It is time we learn and teach that if ever things do not go our way, it is not the ultimate crashing of heaven's dome and whatever comes... Whatever... we always have a better way out than killing ourselves that we have to find out but maybe not "OVER A CUP OF COFFEE" anymore...

Another evening, as I sip my coffee the chocolaty taste melts into my mouth. A thought strikes me with this bitter and sugary flavour that I love so much, why did that man prefer to choose the bitterness and not the sugary aspect? Why was he so lost, so desolate, so full of despair? Among all the old debts that piled on him, was there no one's love to hold him, to keep him from ending his precious life? Being so engrossed in minting money did he overlook the very fact that he and his coffee had been building relationships? Why couldn't he bridge up the gap? Why was there so much of void that he had to give up? Was he torn or lovelorn? Why could he not resort to a loved one because we all know that every time we are lost, every time life seems to be a maze and we stand no hope, no chance; love comes as the last solace to save us from disenchantment and misery.

He ended his life with a few sorry calls but will he ever be able to mend for his family that squalls?

The debts could have been dealt with had he-as a 'fighter' been reborn but nothing can be done now as he, is now gone.

#RIPVGSIDDHARTHA

8. CINDERELLA REVISITED

"Where is my little angel... Where...where... Let me see.... Here she is... Caught you.... " hahaha... and this is how mumma and Magna always played and their laughter echoed in every corner of the house like tinkling of hundreds of tiny bells. The game of hide and seek was just not a game but rather a strong string that kept these two beeds bound close together and Magna had always asked a question after being caught: "How do you find me every time easily, mom?" To which mom only said, "I am a mom, I know it all and wherever you go you will always find me around." These sentences had become as if the prelude to the evening studies session. It was a small happy family of Kolkata and with the "Alpona", "Ponjika", "Kashondi", "Aalta" and "Kashar thala bashon" there was one more thing that was always to be found; that is love. The love of Kaushambhi for her daughter. And while the sounds of their tinkling laughter still echoed the clock struck 4, it was time for Magna's dance class. Draped in her best "taant" saree with crisp pleats and a whiff of the starch, Kaushambhi stepped out yelling at Magna to be quick or else they would miss the tram to her dance class in Gariahaat. Magna stepped out all dressed in her white and red Saree the perfect costume for she was learning the Dhak Dhunuchi dance. Hurriedly, Kaushambhi kissed her daughter, picked up her bunch of keys to lock the main door and as she stepped ahead she saw a car rushing at full speed towards her daughter; in a "Durga avataar" she leapt saving Magna but couldn't be saved herself. People rushed her to the nearby hospital but it had already been too late. The excessive blood flow did not let Kaushambhi survive. Magna was appalled. Her mother was all that she had and now she had been broke as all that she had had, was gone.

Soon, it was time for Durga puja the much awaited festival at Kolkata. The festival of colours, "sindoor khela", "pandaals", "alpana", "korial sarees" but this year's Durga puja was lustreless, barren and insipid for this little girl. She was left all alone. Her mother had left her and "Baudi", the land lady of the two room set where Magna and her mother used to live, had been perspicacious enough to not let Magna continue living there as she knew that now a young girl of 7 will not be able to pay any rent. After all the investigation the police finally handed over Magna to one of the orphanages in Kolkata. As Magna stood at the gate of the orphanage with a big board "Asha foundation" she found it to be no less than a lychgate. Little Magna was in a state of chafe, some unknown fear was gripping her. It was like a new born baby had been taken away from the mother's lap and put into a stranger's arms. Magna wanted to cry her heart out but she only whimpered. She was asked to enter the gate; it sent chills down her pine. The open gate of the orphanage seemed to her like the gaping mouth of a demon and as she entered inside she saw a dense thicket. All trees lined in a row looked to her like the sentinels of the "demon". Utterly petrified she was unable to move as if her legs had been caught in a swamp when she heard the voice of the matron who gently said, "Go to your room child. Room number- 9." Like an obedient docile cow Magna followed her instructions to reach her room. The first thing she did in that small room was to drag the shaky stool to a spot near her bed and place her Mother's picture on it.

This is how her journey at "The Asha Foundation" started. Now it used to be a daily routine of getting up early to get ready by herself where making plaits would be the biggest challenge and Magna was generally seen in a messy unset bun. The breakfast she got at the mess stood nowhere in comparison to the tasty "Radha Ballabhi" and "Koraishutir Kachuri" but whatever she got she ate in her calm muteness. But one thing had gripped her that was fear. She felt tremulous every time she saw the trees near the entrance. There was something that caught her fancy and made her tremble. Don't know if it was the sudden shock of her mother's demise or the loneliness that had created a void within her that made her become so negative. The so called emptiness in her life had no end to it. And as all the kids had made friends and played with each other, Magna had disassociated herself with everything.

One day, Magna watched the kids playing sitting on a distant seat in the field to keep herself as far as possible from the guard of the demon that is the green tree, it started raining. The kids ran to their rooms and so did Magna but she being far away took more time and in this meanwhile, it started pouring heavily. She ran to find some shelter for she hated the large drops of rain that fell on her. After losing her mother Magna hated everything that reminded her of God as for her, had God existed her mother would have existed too. While trying to escape from the heavy rainfall the feet of this little kid slipped and in bewilderment, she held onto something rough, coarse and hard. Regaining her balance she looked up to see that her hand had landed on the rough bark of a huge green tree.   She quickly removed her hand but slipped again on doing so and finally decided to clasp onto the big ebony coloured rough bark. Jerking her short blunt hair to let extra water be shed, she lifted the curly curtains protecting her emerald colour eyes and noticed the tree closely for the first time. It was a prodigious tree with beautiful green leaves and some lovely pretty yellow flowers. The conical green leaves looked glossy as if a fresh coat of colour paint had been used a few minutes back. The yellow flowers did outshine the glittering green. Holding onto the bark carefully maintaining her grip she went to the other side and realised that no rainwater could reach her now to make her drenched. Full of awe, she observed the tree and felt as if it were a mother-fairy spreading its wings of shiny glossy green colour to provide shelter to Magna and save her. She also noticed the yellow flowers which reminded her of Mumma's favourite taant saree which had little yellow flowers embroidered on it. She quickly remembered mumma's statement "Wherever you go, you will always find me around." A soft smile ran across her lips and after a long gap Magna smiled. She understood that Mumma was around and the trees she was always scared of were not guards of any demon but the angels sent by mom. And this gigantic tree that had saved her from falling, she named it "Cindrella". Since that day it was a complete 360 degree turn in Magna's life. Every day, she would take her food from the mess only to come and sit under the tree and eat her meal sharing a bite each day with her dear friend "Cindrella". This very bite that the little Magna would leave behind, would later become a feast for the hungry crows. Magna started enjoying her life at the orphanage. At all times she felt the presence of her beloved mother around. It was from here that Magna developed a particular feeling of love and belongingness towards Nature and grew up to become an environmentalist.

Time flew and she grew up into a smart, confident and independent girl full of humility and love. Magna has been working as an environmentalist for 7 years now where her first save environment project was named "Kaushambhi" and she also got the Goldman Environmental Prize. Even today, she does not forget to visit Cinderella and on being questioned as to how she planned to pick up this profession, she gleefully responds, " Mumma and Cinderella kept guiding me".

It is very true that till the time we are ignorant, we keep missing onto the best things in life. Also people may die leaving the body but the soul never dies. When the bond is strong it stands all the ravages of time to stay forever even after death and destruction.

Magna has also started performing the Dhak Dhunuchi at the Pandaal during the Durga- puja and every time she smells the fragrance of the smoke she feels connected to her mother.

hugs.

9. THE GOOD SAMARITAN

It is not always what it appears to be. We are not always what we feel we are. Yes, life is the most magical thing that happens around us. I wonder if...

I knew Ambrosia since she had been a little girl of three. A sassy brat, she had been known for her antics as a little girl. As she grew getting transformed from a little girl with twinkling eyes to an adolescent who had teeth thrusting themselves out of the mouth, hair so dark that they gave a certain darkling feel to her whole being and a frown always present on the forehead as if it were her permanent crown, she became more acid-tempered. She was snooty and a favorite of all in her group as she was the richest of all. Every time, I saw her with her troupe she was no less than a daughter of Caessars. The whole band of her followers that she had got from amongst her colony mates just for an exchange of a candy or a wafer or her old hairclips were her hard-earned treasure.

I still remember how I would often see her running errands for her mother not because of any affection she had for her mum but rather the love she had for her newly bought bicycle. She was the proud owner of this which her friends had always dreamt of and she took all the fun in showing it off to the whole lot of kids in the colony. I remember how she always used to avoid making an eye contact with me as she flew on her bicycle which appeared to be no less than the "witch's broom" to me, on which she would fly away. Why she was not fond of me was a question I always had in my mind. Whatever be the reason, the fact was that she wasn't very fond of anyone in the whole vicinity.

But we are mighty, frail humans and "Nature" has its own ways of teaching us the ways of life. I will never forget the day when the rain came falling not just to stimulate the caterpillars and build puddles but perhaps also to wash off the negativity and harshness of a few hearts. It was a day when the "Princess" led the contingent on her bicycle and it seemed that she was the queen Juno whose peacocks flew amain to carry her. Not just the palanquin in her bicycle but she had much more to showoff this particular time. Her new blue suede shoes. It was the bribe dad had paid her for not being able to give her much time and she was flaunting them. As her batch of loyalists followed her like docile cows, Ambrosia reached their so called hub, "The Lake Park" which would be their base for next few hours. The only hours in a day when their mothers were free souls at home. Free from the bondage of serving the enfant terrible of the houses. As they occupied the benches and sat with the solemnity of ministers in a court, the orator started. "£ 7000, yes £ 7000, that is what cost my dad to get me these", stormed Ambrosia. The statement came like a news that was no less than Israel attacking Palestine once again and Victor immediately responded, "Daylight robbery, it's mere daylight robbery" while Paul, the real competitor of Victor did not fail in presenting his view; talking about how 'The Renaissance' had impacted the true artists and boot-makers who never compromised on quality. As Roslia could really see the conversation going nowhere, in her cute childish innocence she asked for an opportunity to adorn the suede shoes for 5 minutes. Ambrosia was in complete denial and all could see it on her walnut face which had become pale. Not to forget, the faces of the other girls of the group that were already green tinted. "They are so pricy and precious you see", said Ambrosia "Nobody touches them except for me". This verbal exchange was suddenly interrupted by the winds that started to blow as if sighing at the envy of the green-tinted faces. Within no time the wind turned into a brisk gale and the sky looked pitch dark.

Seeing the weather turning against them, the multitude decided to rush back home and thus headed towards their bicycles. As they stepped ahead they heard a sound as that of a sudden strike on one of the piano keys. They moved further and with every step the sound became louder. It was whimpering and whining and the sound restricted their movement. As they stood stunned knowing not what to do, to their utter surprise Ambrosia followed the sound and headed towards a drain that had been there for years of course, unnoticed for the little lot. "The sound is from the drain", shouted Ambrosia

"What are you all waiting for? Step up! We need help." Her words came as a war cry in the battlefield from the king and all reached the drain area like obedient soldiers. But before they could do much the sky poured down all it had and the drain was half full of water. "What should we do?", while the others kept mulling Ambrosia bent to take a clear look of the drain. Floating in water came a little puppy crying, yelping for help. She immediately scooped it up with both her hands and handed it over to Victor. The others got busy in trying to look for a little dry place and in no time Ambrosia shoved her hands into the sloppy, viscous and foul water of the drain but unable to spot anymore, within no time she entered the drain and was submerged in dirty water till the calf muscles. What happened after this was no less than the miracles of Jesus shown in Mark's Gospel. It was a great struggle as she kept lifting puppies out of the already brimming mucky water of the drain. One after the other, the crew saved six puppies in a row and then Ambrosia stepped out. Finally, managing her scarf that lay under the raincoat in her bag she got the puppies placed on one of the benches under a tree with the help of her friends. She stood there taking a deep breath while the others had a weird expression on their faces which is generally seen when some mischief of the nasty kids is discovered by the parents. While she stood there, all stared at her. Stunned by their piercing gaze she looked down, to her horror her blue suede shoes were now mucky and not blue anymore. Stained by the mud in the drain and the rainy water, they had now turned brown. All stood expecting Ambrosia to howl in anger but all that was heard was a euphonious voice of the brown puppy present in the litter. She immediately turned towards it and patted it while it licked the hands of its SAVIOUR. They had a certain gleam in their eyes. All six of them. A gleam of purity of heart, love or maybe gratitude. The storm had calmed by now so the kids called out to the park watchman and arranged for a big carton box which was the then makeshift accommodation of the little angels who came to this earth not with wings but with whiskers and paws. It was now time for the whole group to return to the pavilion where their worried and furious mothers would not really welcome them for they were all shabby and drenched.

Finally, they hopped on to their bicycles and rode back home; once again the leader led the cyclers but this time the look on her face was different. Her eyes were as candid as that of the little innocent puppies. The wind seemed to caress her as she rode. Her suede shoes were all stained but these were not stains they rather were medals of victory that she carried triumphantly. The spongy roadside was twilled and the yellow flowers of the bushes seemed to smile at the horde. Drenched, as they were, they looked no less than chaste nymphs that had just appeared out of their crisp channels. They rode past me and for the first time Ambrosia looked at me wishing a "Hello Ms. Pandey" her wish made me curious I knew by instinct of a lady that something had happened. Something different. Something magical. I wished her back instructing her to ride safely to which she responded "Aye, Aye Captain!" but that day it wasn't me it was her who was the victorious Captain of a ship that had got stuck in a great storm but was brought ashore by this girl with indomitable spirit.

And as I said at the beginning, "I wonder if it was her loneliness that made her a grim visaged girl or it was her inherent goodness that made her venture into the arduous task of being the SAVIOUR keeping up with her name "AMBROSIA" conferring longevity upon the little creatures..." I still wonder what it was but yes, Mother Nature took its course to teach a priceless lesson to her children and stood by the ones who though were not humans but belonged to Her.

As far as "The Lake Park" is concerned, it is still their favourite haunt but now the gang has grown bigger and there are watch-DOGS, ensuring safety of the kids as they play.

When not pawned,
Love goes BEYOND...

10. BEYOND…

Dear Guddu,

Hope you are doing fine. I am writing just to ask if I stand a chance at all to see you... to meet you... for maybe once in this lifetime just for once...

It was around 15 years after parting ways that he had written to her. But why did he? What for? Was there anything that was still left? These words echoed deep in her mind as Guddu grabbed the letter from the office clerk's hand who had been a little sceptical after receiving the letter and had been curious while handing it over. Guddu was in her early 30s and was one of the prettiest teachers at school. Pretty not just because she was young but because she had a pure heart and people admired her for that. This was the first time she had received a mail at school and that too from an anonymous sender. The very instant she had held the letter she knew it was from "the old man". Well, that is what she used to call him then to tease him. What made her know it came from him was the way the address was written. In the address her full name with the changed surname that she had acquired post marriage, along with the vermillion, bangles and toe-ring, was also written the nickname in brackets *(Guddu)*. Who else could have addressed her by that name? As she walked through the empty corridors holding herself carefully to ensure that she didn't break or fall weak, she remembered those days when she was a bubbly teenager waiting for her class 12 results. It was then that she had met him. He being her brother's friend had visited her house as they came on a professional tour. She remembered how she had then cursed the unknown visitor for whom she had had to get up early in the morning to ensure presenting a well-set house and prepare a tasty meal for lunch. Those days were different the daughters of working mothers matured apace. So at the age of 17, she knew it all from cleaning to cooking to decorating the house and setting the ambience to ensure the guest to feel comfortable and warm; and she was paying the price for the same. Not to forget, the fellow visiting was to be a grade one officer in next six months with the government and the regard should be kept up. The flashback paused as her thoughts were interrupted by a sweet wish from a grade 9 girl.

As the teacher overpowered, Guddu who had been born at the very view of that letter in a pink envelope, died. The grade 9 girl who looked chirpy, happy and pretty was almost like what Guddu had looked then. Reaching the staff room, she quietly slipped the envelope in her bag and got busy with her fellow teachers. ". But why did he? What for? Was there anything that was still left?" these very thoughts came knocking again and again and finally, when she was all by herself, she took out the envelope and read the letter. It wasn't very surprising for her to see that how the whole page had just a salutation and 2 lines written. Very much like their relationship, the page was blank and moreover, he had always been a man of few words. Even then it had been she who kept on talking non-stop. But now she was a solemn woman. Or maybe then she was so happy to be with him that she couldn't help but talk.

As she read the letter, she knew not what she should be feeling. She was not happy! She was not sad! She was rather numb. What struck her was not that the man who had always meant the life to her wanted to meet her but rather a thought that what could have made him write to her, was he ok or not. She immediately picked the phone and dialed 9415767475.... But stopped midway. "He would hang up on her like always, why should she call him?", she thought to herself and continued with her work. As she tried with all her mite to not think of him and the letter, she heard the contraltos of the music lesson being conducted by the music teacher.

I will be there for you

Even if the days are few

For now and forever

I will leave you never

I will be your magic wand

Cuz it's not just love, it's BEYOND...

As the words of the song resonated, a realization smote her. It was this that she had promised him every time she had seen him, every time she had thought of him, with every gaze she had exchanged as he had appeased his hunger that day praising the meal cooked by her, with every bite and with every stroke of pink that was seen on her cheeks as she had blushed then. She remembered how her heart had danced to the tunes of her ringing telephone every time she got a call after his call on which he had expressed his love to her. She remembered how her eyes had searched for him on the crowded streets when she had once visited his hometown. The search which had been futile. But who could have argued with the heart of a young girl in love that did beat as fast as a galloping horse's steps.

So many memories just so many of them it seemed that somebody had opened a fisc and placed all the riches on the table. It all flashed before her eyes and in that very moment, she typed a message unblocking his number:

Dear Old man

Hope you are fine...

Yes, we can meet at the same old café tomorrow at 4pm.

She had been careful enough in not typing more than 2 sentences with a salutation. That whole evening she was a little uneasy. She reached home from school and looked at her family. It was a long non-verbal communication she had with them ensuring them of her loyalty. She knew that the family was her hard-earned wealth as in every arranged marriage set up the girl comes as an outsider and winning over the family members to make them all hers was no less than winning a match against Germany at the FIFA World Cup. She had done it and she owned them now with love, affection and a sense of belongingness. There were no words but yet a lot was said as she had looked at her husband and peeped deep into his eyes; eyes that were the coppice gate that led one to his soul and this exchange of ideas with no presence of words gave her an extraordinary confidence.

The next day she reached the café with a fear stinging her heart. How would she even recognise him? She had seen him only twice and that too 15 years ago. She sat at one of the tables and ordered for a black coffee which had been her all time favorite and she remembered how her husband would always ask her that what made her like the insipid coffee to which she had always replied that he brought so much of sweetness in her life that she needed the insipid coffee to balance it. A sweet smile ran across her lips; it was a pure smile rather. A smile that is seen on the faces of little girls as they admire their Barbie. A smile of contentment.

She then saw him approaching; not a minute she took in recognizing him. Yes, it was him. The one who broke her heart. The one who made her sad. She quickly covered these thoughts of malice with a fake smile and waved at him. "Hi", he said in a guttural tone, reaching the table here she sat. "I am so happy you agreed to meet me", before he could say anything further her phone beeped. It was her daughter. She took the call and answered the million dollar question as to when mum would reach back home. It took her some 5 minutes to finish the call and all this while he kept quiet waiting patiently like a monk. Finishing up the call she looked at him. "How've you been?', she asked and before she could get an answer the phone screen flashed HUBBY Calling... it took her another 10 minutes in helping him out by giving directions as to the best flowers to be picked for a bouquet that he could give to his boss. As she kept giving directions over the call the love lorn "old man" kept looking at her. How beautiful she looked in a simple blue saree, a small bindi on her forehead, the locks of her loosely tied hair hanging down from behind her ears, her little earrings that shook in agreement to every word of hers and the "mangalsutra" in her neck. The last piece of her jewellery brought his world to a standstill and as she finished the directions over the call, he called out to the waiter for the bill. Clearing the bill he thanked her for taking out time to meet him and told her that he only wanted to see her as he was in town. Next, he seeked permission to leave and left her in a fix. She drove back home thinking that it was a pleasant meeting and thanked God that all was right.

Two days later, she received another letter at her school, this time in a white envelope. As she opened the envelope, the letter read

Dear Madam,

It was a pleasure meeting you that day. I shall forever be thankful. As I saw you that day I realized that you have grown prettier and as I overheard you conversation with your family members I felt happy to know that you are happy. Yes, I came to try my luck once again but there is a slight problem; that day I went to meet Guddu though I met some other lady who does not belong to me. Yes, I love Guddu and I shall forever do that but I do not intend to disturb anybody else's life. I am sorry for the trouble I caused.

With warm regards and blessings

Col Bisht.

She was surprised! It was a letter from him. It was his writing. And she could not speak a word. She just had crystal, luminous drops of tear rolling down her cheeks. He may have been the one who broke her heart but it was He who saved her family from breaking. Perhaps He had loved her so much that He came looking for her after so many years and still He loved her enough to let her go. Her love which she always felt to be very strong, pure, platonic, giving seemed so small today because what He had for her was much more than love. It was BEYOND...